The Year of the Rat

Tales from the Chinese Zodiac

Written by Oliver Chin
Illustrated by Miah Alcorn

immedium
Immedium, Inc.
San Francisco

The following day,
the dog lost his leash.

Next, the bucket dropped
into the well, and Bing's
kite wouldn't fly.

He discovered the reason why,
and poor Ralph promised, "I will
keep my mouth to myself."

But Bing's parents had enough. Their son's birthday party was tomorrow, and they didn't want any more problems from that little rat. They told a disappointed Bing to bring Ralph to the barn.

Putting Ralph in the rabbit cage, Bing whispered,
"If you're good and stay here, you can go home tomorrow."

Ralph twitched his nose
sadly as Bing shut the
door and waved goodbye.

Outside the barn door, Ralph saw Bing's neighbors decorate the street. He smelled cakes baking and heard people laughing.

Ralph moaned, "Oh, I wish I could join the party, too!"

Finally Bing's birthday had come, and so did family and friends. Presents arrived along with a big bunch of balloons. They sparkled like every color of the rainbow.

Bing wanted to touch them all,

but suddenly their knot came loose.

Fearing that the balloons would fly away, he snatched their strings. "Whew!" he sighed. However, the bunch kept pulling him up!

When his feet could no longer touch the ground, Bing shouted, "Oh, rats!"

Everybody turned and gasped in alarm. Quickly they tried to grab hold of him, but he slipped through their grasp.

Ralph heard Bing's cry. He looked out the window as his friend rose slowly into the air beyond the reach of man and beast.

"I'll help you!"
Ralph squealed, but the cage door was locked tight.

Ralph anxiously scoured the floor for anything useful. Then he rummaged through his pockets. **A-ha!** He found a pin, reached around the bars, and jiggled the lock open. **He was free!**

The rat bolted through a hole in the wall and scaled the ladder to the hayloft. Bing kept floating higher and higher.

On the ledge, Ralph took a deep breath, closed his eyes, and jumped out!

Boing! Boing! Resting on top of the bouncing balloons, Ralph called down, **"Are you alright, Bing?"**

The boy looked up with amazement and grinned, "Ralph, I'm glad to see you!"

Scratching his head, Ralph squeaked,
"What should I do?"

They had soared above the trees
and now could almost touch the
clouds. Bing hollered, "I don't know,
but think of something!"

Suddenly Ralph got an idea. He carefully squeezed in between the balloons.

Next, he slid down the cords to Bing's hands.

Then he began to bite through the strings like a pair of scissors!

One after another, the balloons flew away, and the pair descended slowly towards the earth. In the mean time, they had drifted far from home.

Ralph decided, "I think I see a place where we can safely land."

He had eight twisty, twirly arms,
and he loved to use them to tickle.

When Octopus tickled the little fish, they
jumped and jiggled and wriggled and giggled!
They thought tickling was tons of fun!

But most of the creatures found his tickling tiresome. Octopus tickled Sea Star and made her squirm. "Stop it!" she squeaked.

Octopus tickled clickety-clackety Crab, and Crab tripped and tumbled into the sand.

"Go away!" he snapped.

„Aber wie lang ist denn eine winzige, kurze Stunde? Ist sie lang oder
kurz?", ruft Lotte. „Wenn du dich langweilst, ist sie lang, und wenn
du dich nicht langweilst, ist sie kurz!", ruft ihre Mutter zurück.

„Ich langweile mich aber!", schreit Lotte wütend. „Und ich will,
dass die Stunde jetzt sofort vorbei ist!"

Gelangweilt wirft Lotte sich auf den Teppich im Wohnzimmer
und starrt den alten chinesischen Schrank an, auf den
ein Drache aufgemalt ist: ein grüner Drache mit einem langen
grünen Drachenschwanz, der sein Maul aufreißt. Er hat
eine feuerrote lange Zunge und vier spitze Zähne, aber wirklich
gefährlich wirkt er nicht, denn er klimpert treuherzig mit
seinen langen Wimpern. Er klimpert? Tatsächlich! Seine Augen
bewegen sich und dann sein langer Schwanz, und da kriecht
er auch schon auf seinen großen Tatzen langsam vom Schrank
hinunter auf Lotte zu.

„Hallo?", sagt Lotte vorsichtig.

„Ni hau", sagt der Drache.

„Ni hau", wiederholt Lotte langsam.

„Sehr gut", sagt der Drache, „du sprichst ja chinesisch. ‚Ni hau'
heißt auf Chinesisch ‚guten Tag'. Schön, dich kennenzulernen!
Ich langweile mich nämlich so."

„Du langweilst dich?", fragt Lotte erstaunt.
„Ja, möchtest du vielleicht von morgens bis abends
auf einem alten Schrank sitzen?", fragt der Drache,
dreht sich auf den Rücken und streckt seine
Drachentatzen in die Luft.

„Kraul mich mal", sagt er.
Lotte tippt dem Drachen vorsichtig auf seinen
schuppigen Drachenbauch.

„Mehr!", sagt der Drache. Lotte krault ihm den Bauch.
„Hm, das ist schön", knurrt der Drache. „Scheeschee.
Das heißt ‚danke' auf Chinesisch."

Der Drache krabbelt vom Teppich und läuft in die Küche.
„Wo willst du denn hin?", ruft Lotte.
„Hunger", knurrt der Drache, „ich habe grässlichen Hunger."
Was mag ein chinesischer Drache wohl essen?
Lotte findet ein Päckchen Glasnudeln im Vorratsschrank und
ein paar chinesische Suppen. „Magst du das?"
„Ich will Schokoladenpudding!", brüllt der Drache und legt
sich vor den Kühlschrank.

GLÜCKS-KEKSE

ESSIG

ÖL

GLAS-NUDELN

HOF

WOK SAUCE

PASTA

YOGI-TEE

Lotte gibt ihm einen Schokoladenpudding.
„Scheeschee", sagt der Drache und mit seiner
langen Drachenzunge schlabbert er den Pudding
im Handumdrehen weg.

Befriedigt rülpst er. Dabei kommt eine große Flamme aus seinem
Maul.

„Achtung", ruft Lotte, „dass du nichts anzündest!"

„Keine Angst", sagte der Drache, „das war nur mein Feueratem,
da spucke ich hinterher und der zündet nichts an. So, und jetzt
machen wir einen Drachentanz."

„Einen was?", fragt Lotte, aber da watschelt der Drache schon
zurück ins Wohnzimmer.

Der Drache zerrt die rote Decke mit seinen Zähnen vom Sofa.

„Die Decke hängst du dir jetzt über den Kopf", sagt er, „denn das
ist dein Drachenkopf, und auf die Finger klebst du dir lange Papier-
schnipsel, das sind deine Drachenkrallen, und die Zunge streckst
du so weit raus, wie du kannst, und dann fauchst du."

„Bekomme ich dann auch einen Feueratem?", fragt Lotte.

„Nein", sagt der Drache, „weil deine Mutter kein Drache ist, bekommst
du keinen. Aber du bist jetzt meine kleine Drachenschwester und
zusammen machen wir den Drachentanz. Alles klar?"

„Ja", sagt Lotte, „alles klar." Sie klebt sich mit Uhu Zeitungsschnipsel
auf die Fingernägel, hängt sich die rote Decke über den Kopf,
streckt die Zunge raus und kriecht auf allen vieren dem Drachen
hinterher.

It was the best scare
she'd ever had.